The Winter's Tale

Sweet Cherry

Published by Sweet Cherry Publishing Limited
Unit 36, Vulcan House,
Vulcan Road,
Leicester, LE5 3EF
United Kingdom

First published in the UK in 2012
2020 edition

4 6 8 10 9 7 5 3

ISBN: 978-1-78226-001-1

© Macaw Books

The Winter's Tale

Based on the original story by William Shakespeare,
adapted by Macaw Books.
Lexile® code numerical measure L = Lexile® 1110L

Guided Reading Level = T

Cover design and illustrations by Macaw Books

www.sweetcherrypublishing.com

Printed and bound in China
C.GD.012

About *Shakespeare*

William Shakespeare, regarded as the greatest writer in the English language, was born in Stratford-upon-Avon in Warwickshire, England (around 23 April 1564). He was the third of eight children born to John and Mary Shakespeare.

Shakespeare was a poet, playwright and dramatist. He is often known as England's national poet and the 'Bard of Avon'. Thirty-eight plays, one hundred and fifty-four sonnets, two long narrative poems and several other poems are attributed to him. Shakespeare's plays have been translated into every major existent language and are performed more often than those of any other playwright.

Hermione: She is the beautiful and faithful wife of King Leontes. She is wrongly accused by her husband of having an affair with Polixenes, King of Bohemia. She dies of grief in the play, but is restored to life at the end.

Polixenes: He is the King of Bohemia and childhood friend of Leontes. He is wrongfully accused of having an affair with Hermione, Leontes' wife. He somehow manages to escape Sicily when Leontes plots to kill him.

Leontes: He is the King of Sicily. He has jealous fantasies and is convinced that his wife, Hermione, is having an affair with his childhood friend, Polixenes, who is the King of Bohemia. He acts cruelly towards his wife and later repents of his actions.

Shepherd: He is an old man and a
good natured, honourable shepherd.
He raises Perdita, whom he finds
as a baby, as his own daughter.

The Winter's Tale

Once upon a time, Sicily was ruled by a wise and able king called Leontes. He had a very beautiful and virtuous wife by the name of Hermione. Hermione was such

a gentle and loving wife that
Leontes hardly had any reason
for complaint. She took care of
his every need, but there was
one thing that was missing in
his life – a reunion with his old
childhood friend Polixenes, who
was now the King of Bohemia.

They had been very close friends from birth, but after the death of their fathers, the boys had become deeply involved with their respective kingdoms and, in time, lost touch. After many requests and messages sent, Polixenes agreed to visit Sicily all the way from Bohemia.

Leontes was overjoyed to see his dear old friend again after such a long time. He introduced him to Hermione and the three of them would spend long hours chatting with each other, the two old friends recounting tales of their youth to the gentle Hermione.

Soon it was time for Polixenes to return to his kingdom.

Hermione joined her husband in entreating their honoured guest to stay a little while longer. However, this is when the problems started. Polixenes turned down the offer of staying when his own dear friend Leontes begged him, but when Hermione asked him for the same favour, he agreed to her proposal at once.

Leontes was suddenly overcome by a spate of jealousy. He did not know how he should

feel about what was happening. On top of that, Hermione's attention towards Polixenes, which she was continuing to give on the request of her husband, did not go down well with Leontes.

After this had gone on for some time, Leontes became a changed man. Once a caring and loving husband and friend, he had turned into a savage monster. Unable to bear the pangs of jealousy that he now had to face, Leontes sent for one of his lords at court, a man called Camillo, and ordered him to poison Polixenes.

But Camillo was a good man and he knew that what his king had asked him to do was wrong. So, instead of poisoning Polixenes, he informed the King of Bohemia about the plan. Together, they planned to escape from Sicily. Thus, with the help of Camillo, Polixenes was able to return

to his kingdom of Bohemia
safely. He then appointed
Camillo at his court, and soon
Camillo became the king's
best friend and chief advisor.

Back in Sicily, Polixenes'
flight had greater repercussions

than anyone could have
imagined. Infuriated that
the villain who had tried to
woo his wife was still safe
and sound, Leontes decided
to take up the matter with
Hermione. He stormed into her
chambers and, sending their son

Mamillius away, immediately
imprisoned his own wife.

Mamillius was
very fond of his mother
and could not bear to
see her dishonoured
in this way. He was
so grief-stricken that
he stopped eating and
soon it seemed that the
young prince might die.

Meanwhile, Leontes
sent two of his lords at
court, Cleomenes and
Dion, to the Oracle
of Apollo, and asked
Delphos to find out
if his wife had been
unfaithful. Meanwhile,
Hermione gave birth to

a little girl, the newborn child her only comfort in prison.

Now, Hermione had a very good friend called Paulina, the wife of Lord Antigonus at the court of Leontes. Hearing that

Hermione had given birth to a baby girl, Paulina immediately rushed to the prison and asked Emilia, the lady who was taking care of Hermione and the baby, to tell the queen that she wanted to have the baby given to her. She declared that she would take the baby to the father, and perhaps the sight of the newborn child would soften his heart. She also told Emilia to inform the queen that she would defend her in the highest manner possible.

Paulina, with the little baby
in her arms, forced her way into
the court. Her husband tried to
stop her, fearing that this would
only enrage the king,
but Paulina would not listen
to anyone. Presenting herself

before the king, she placed the little baby at his feet. She went on to tell him how he had wrongly imprisoned his devoted wife and begged him

to release her from prison.
But her entire demonstration
only served to anger the king
further, and he immediately
asked Antigonus to take his
wife away from the court.

The minute Paulina left,
Leontes called Antigonus
and asked him to take the
little baby and leave it in the
desert to perish. Antigonus
was no Camillo and did just
as his king had ordered. He
immediately took the baby

away, intending to leave her in the first desert he could find.

Leontes was now seething for reasons beyond anyone's understanding. He could not wait for his two lords to return from the Oracle and gave Hermione a public trial, wanting to issue her with a just punishment for her folly. When everyone had gathered around poor Hermione, who was now a prisoner before them, both Cleomenes and

Dion entered the court with
the Oracle's declaration. It

stated, "Hermione is innocent, Polixenes blameless – Camillo is a true subject, Leontes a jealous tyrant, and the king shall live without an heir if she who is lost be not found."

Leontes was so headstrong that he found the Oracle to be false and asked the jury present to proceed with their judgment on the prisoner. Just at that moment, a man entered the assembly and declared that the young prince Mamillius, upon hearing that his mother was being tried for a crime she did not commit, had died of shock.

Hearing the news of the
death of her son, Hermione

fainted. Leontes felt sorry for his wife and asked her attendants

to take her away and try to revive her. But Paulina soon returned to the assembly and informed the king that Hermione was indeed dead.

It was only then that Leontes repented his cruelty towards his wife. He knew that her heart was pure and she was indeed innocent. He also realised

that if his daughter were left
in the desert, then the Oracle
would be proved right and
he would be left heirless.

Meanwhile, as these
thoughts were going through

the king's mind, Antigonus,
after being caught in a storm,
had been redirected towards
Bohemia. He arrived on the
coast of Bohemia and carried out
the king's orders. Leaving the

baby there, he was about to turn back and leave for Sicily when a bear emerged from behind the bushes and tore him apart.

A poor shepherd, walking along the coast, came across the baby. He saw that she was dressed in rich clothes and jewels,

and a scrap of paper was tied
to her arm which read 'Perdita'.
Being a kind man, the shepherd
took the baby with him. His
wife was overjoyed to see the
baby. The shepherd used the

jewellery to buy many sheep and
goats, and soon, he became very
rich. He raised Perdita as his
own and she came to be known
as the shepherd's daughter.

Now, Polixenes had a young son called Florizel. One day, when Florizel was walking in the palace grounds, he saw the beautiful Perdita and immediately fell in love with her. He did not tell her that he was a prince, but instead introduced himself as Doricles, a gentleman who lived nearby. They soon became very good friends.

One day, Polixenes sent some people to follow Florizel, as he wanted to know where

his son went every day. When
the men came back and told
the king what they had seen,
the king and Camillo decided
to pay the shepherd a visit,
dressed as mere travellers.

Festivities were being held
at the shepherd's house, and the
king and Camillo were warmly
welcomed. As they joined in with
the celebrations, they noticed
Florizel and Perdita sitting in a

corner. Rather than dancing and feasting, they sat quietly in each other's company. The king admitted that he had never seen a prettier girl in his life and Camillo could not help but comment, "Truly, she is the queen of curds and cream."

But then Polixenes revealed his true self and ordered his son never to see the

shepherd's daughter again, or
else he would have the girl and
her father killed. As Polixenes
left in a huff, Camillo, who
had been enamoured by
Perdita's beauty, asked the
two lovers to leave for Sicily
and take shelter in the court
of King Leontes. So Florizel,
Perdita and the old shepherd
made haste for Sicily. The
shepherd even took the clothes
and the note he had found
on the infant with him.

When the two love-struck
youths reached Leontes' court,
he welcomed them warmly. He
immediately developed a deep
affection for Perdita, whose

appearance reminded him of his own wife Hermione. Looking at Perdita, he said, "Such a sweet creature my daughter might have been, if I had not cruelly sent her from me."

Hearing the king speak these words, the shepherd at once realised that Perdita was none other than the daughter Leontes

spoke of. He immediately
showed the king the clothes
and the piece of paper, and it

was ascertained that Perdita was indeed his long-lost daughter. The king was beside himself with joy and rewarded the shepherd handsomely for bringing his daughter back to him.

Polixenes, on learning that the girl he had forbidden his son from marrying was none other than the daughter of his dear friend, at once consented to the marriage. But even though everyone in the courts of both Sicily and Bohemia were very happy about the alliance, Leontes was sad when he remembered the harsh treatment he had meted out to his wife many years ago

and that Hermione could not share with him this joyous day.

Paulina, who was now in high favour with the king, came over to Leontes and said that she had created a life-like statue of Hermione, and

now that everything was fine
again she wanted to present it
to him. So Paulina, Florizel,
Perdita and Leontes all set off
towards Paulina's house, where
the statue was shown to them.

Truly, never had there been a more life-like statue built of any person as the one that stood before them. While everyone present praised its beauty, Leontes remained silent; he could not bring himself to say anything. But after a while, he mentioned that unlike the statue, Hermione had few wrinkles on her face. Perdita interjected and said that perhaps the sculptor wanted to show them how she would look had she still been alive.

Paulina told the king that it
might be better if she drew the
curtains back over the statue,
as he seemed visibly pale. But
Leontes wanted to stare at the

statue for a while longer. Paulina
replied that if the king were to do
so, he might think it was alive.

At that moment, the statue
stepped off its pedestal and

walked up to the king, threw
her arms around him and kissed
him. Hermione had not died
after all! She had been kept in
hiding by her faithful friend,
Paulina. And although she had

learnt earlier that the king had repented his follies, she could not bring herself to show herself to him until she received news about her daughter. But now that Perdita had been found, she forgave her husband.

Perdita and Florizel were
married, and in a way it was
like a second marriage for
Leontes and Hermione. After
all those years, Leontes was
finally able to get the peace
he so desperately wanted.